Meet
Strawberry Shortcake

Illustrated by Lisa Workman

Grosset & Dunlap • New York

ISBN 0-448-43132-7   A B C D E F G H I J
Special Markets ISBN 0-448-43705-8

It was a special day in Strawberryland—Apple Dumplin's berry first birthday!

"Happy Birthday, Apple Dumplin'!" said Strawberry Shortcake. "To celebrate, we're going to have a party. But first we have some shopping to do!"

Strawberry made a list:
COOKIES
FRUIT
JUICE
PARTY HATS
BIRTHDAY CAKE

Strawberry Shortcake brought her map.
"We have to take the Berry Trail," she said. "And it looks like we'll have to travel to some berry, berry interesting lands to find everything we need."

"Is there a place on your map where folks meow and purr?" asked Custard.

"We'll have more fun if we meet different kinds of people," Strawberry replied. "The world would be a berry, berry boring place if we were all alike!"

Before long, they reached a village that smelled like warm cookies!

"Yummy!" Apple cried.

"This must be Cookie Corners," said Strawberry Shortcake. "We should have a berry easy time finding cookies here!"

Just then, the door of a bakery opened and a girl rolled out a cart full of cookies. Pupcake was so excited, he ran right into her. Cookies flew everywhere!

"Oh macaroonio!" the girl exclaimed. She looked very upset.

"I'm sorry," Strawberry Shortcake said. "Pupcake gets really excited when he meets new people."

"Woof!" barked Pupcake. Then he licked the girl's face.

She giggled. "That's okay. Hi, I'm Ginger Snap," she said.

Ginger Snap took them inside her bakery. There they saw the most amazing cookie-making machine! It even made a tuna macaroon for Custard.

"A tuna cookie? Now that's really different," Strawberry Shortcake said.

"Different, but delicious," the cat purred.

Soon the girls were loading the pink wagon with cookies. Strawberry Shortcake was berry, berry happy—not just to have cookies, but a new friend as well!

She waved good-bye to Ginger Snap, then looked at her map. "Now we need to find fruit and juice. Next stop, Orange Blossom Acres!"

In Orange Blossom Acres, they saw a girl picking fruit in an orchard.

"Hi. I'm Strawberry Shortcake," Strawberry told the girl. "And this is my sister, Apple Dumplin'."

"I'm Orange Blossom," the girl said.

Strawberry told Orange Blossom about the party.
"Please take as much juice as you want, and fruit, too.
I've got plenty!" Orange Blossom said with a laugh.
Strawberry Shortcake thanked her new friend,
and got back on the Berry Trail.

The next town was made of giant cakes.
"No wonder it's called Cakewalk!" Strawberry Shortcake exclaimed. They walked into a store called Angel Cake's Cake Shoppe.

APPLE CAKE
RECIPE

"Hi, I'm Angel Cake," said the girl behind the counter.
"Can I help you?"

She showed them photos of all kinds of cakes.
Apple cooed when she saw a cake covered in apples.

"This is the one!" Strawberry said. "We'll need it by
this afternoon."

"That's impossible!" Angel said. "It's too much work
for one person."

"What if we all work together?" Strawberry Shortcake suggested. "If you get the recipe, I can help you gather the ingredients. I'll pour. Apple will mix. Custard can clean up— and Pupcake can nap!"

Finally, the cake was done. "This was hard work," Strawberry Shortcake said, "but because we worked together, it was actually fun!"

Custard licked the counter clean. "I wouldn't go that far."

"Only a special cat could help the way you have," Angel said.

Custard purred.

Their next stop was Upper Hat Rack. But after walking for a while, Strawberry Shortcake checked the map and sighed. "We're berry, berry lost."

Just then, a pony trotted up to them. "I, Honey Pie Pony, am an expert in giving directions. Have you tried north? Or south? Or east? What about west? Then there's northeast and..."

"Could you tell us the way to Upper Hat Rack?" Strawberry Shortcake asked.

"One of my favorite places, like Upper Coat Rack, but less crowded. I'll take you there!" the chatty pony replied.

Soon they were even more lost, and in a dark, scary forest!
Suddenly, Pupcake barked and ran ahead.
"Pupcake, wait!" Strawberry cried. She ran after Pupcake.
But Pupcake tumbled through a leaf-covered door.
He landed right in the arms of a strange boy!

"Hello, who are you?" Strawberry Shortcake asked the boy.

"Huckleberry Pie's my name. But you can call me Huck," the boy said. "And this is my fort, in the heart of Huckleberry Briar," he added proudly.

Strawberry Shortcake looked around. "That's a berry fine spyglass you have," she said.

"Want to take a peek?" Huck offered.

Strawberry looked through the glass. She saw a river made of chocolate. Huck offered to take them there.

The friends made their way through the thick woods.
"I almost forgot!" Strawberry Shortcake exclaimed.
"We need to get to Upper Hat Rack for party hats!"
"Oh, that's miles from here," Huck said. "But how about this?" Huck quickly twisted vines and berries into beautiful little hats.

Finally they arrived at the River Fudge. Pupcake was so excited, he ran in circles, jumping on and off the wagon. One big jump knocked the handle right out of Strawberry Shortcake's hand.

The wagon rolled toward the river—with Apple Dumplin' in it!

"Uh-oh!" Apple cried in alarm.

Strawberry leaped onto Honey's back. "Giddy up!" she shouted.

Custard scrambled up a tree, then dropped onto the pony's back, too.

Strawberry Shortcake pulled a vine from her party hat.
Just before the wagon could roll into the river, she looped the vine
around the handle and pulled with all her might. The wagon teetered
on the edge of the chocolate stream, then stopped!

Strawberry Shortcake ran over and scooped up Apple Dumplin'. The baby was safe, but the wagon kept rolling! The party supplies bounced right out. Then the empty wagon fell into the river and floated away.

"Well, Apple and the party supplies are safe. But how will we get them home without the wagon?" Strawberry Shortcake wondered.

"I know just the way," said Huck. He told them his plan, and everyone got to work.

"There's nothing like a raft to get you across a river," Strawberry said. "And nothing like working together to get the job done."

"I never realized how much fun it was to work with others," Huck added.

"Me either," said Custard, surprised.

They loaded the raft and waved good-bye.

Back in Strawberryland, Strawberry Shortcake had everything she needed for the party—except guests! She quickly solved that problem by inviting all their new friends.

Huckleberry Pie, Honey Pie, Orange Blossom, Angel Cake, and Ginger Snap all came to wish Apple Dumplin' "A Berry Happy Birthday."

Everyone had a wonderful time, even Custard. Not one of their new friends had whiskers, but that didn't matter.

"Parties really are more fun when you have all different kinds of guests," the cat admitted.

Strawberry Shortcake laughed. "Custard, I couldn't agree more!"